SuperHero School

Alien Attack!

Also by Alan MacDonald

The Superhero School series:
The Revenge of the Green Meanie

The Troll Trouble series:
Trolls Go Home!
Trolls United
Trolls On Hols
Goat Pie

The History of Warts series:
Custardly Wart: Pirate (third class)
Ditherus Wart: (accidental) Gladiator
Honesty Wart: Witch Hunter!
Sir Bigwart: Knight of the Wonky Table

SUPERHERO SCHOOL

Alien Attack!

Alan MacDonald

Illustrated by Nigel Baines

BLOOMSBURY

LONDON NEW DELHI NEW YORK SYDNEY

Bloomsbury Publishing, London, New Delhi, New York and Sydney

First published in Great Britain in April 2015 by Bloomsbury Publishing Plc
50 Bedford Square, London WC1B 3DP

www.bloomsbury.com

Bloomsbury is a registered trademark of Bloomsbury Publishing Plc

A CIP catalogue record for this book is available from the British Library

ISBN 978 1 4088 2524 2

Printed and bound in Great Britain by CPI Group (UK) Ltd, Croydon CR0 4YY

1 3 5 7 9 10 8 6 4 2

MEET THE SUPERHEROES OF MIGHTY HIGH...

DANGERBOY (aka Stan)

SPECIAL POWERS: Radar ears that sense danger

WEAPON OF CHOICE: Tiddlywinks

STRENGTHS: Survival against the odds

WEAKNESSES: Never stops worrying

SUPER RATING: 53

FRISBEE KID (aka Minnie)

SPECIAL POWERS: Deadly aim

WEAPON OF CHOICE: 'Frisbee anyone?'

STRENGTHS: Organised, bossy

WEAKNESSES: See above

SUPER RATING: 56

BRAINIAC (aka Miles)

SPECIAL POWERS: Super brainbox

WEAPON OF CHOICE: Quiz questions

STRENGTHS: Um . . .

WEAKNESSES: Hates to fight

SUPER RATING: 41.3

PUDDING THE WONDERDOG

SPECIAL POWERS: Sniffing out treats

WEAPON OF CHOICE: Licking and slobbering

STRENGTHS: Obedience

WEAKNESSES: World-class wimp

SUPER RATING: 2

DEEP IN THE DARKEST SPACE A SPACESHIP HURTLES TOWARDS PLANET EARTH ...

Chapter 1
Bionic Bubblegum

Meanwhile, back on Planet Earth, the trainee superheroes of Mighty High were on an exciting school trip with their head teacher.

'Well, this is it,

The Annual Superhero Fan Convention,'

said Miss Marbles, leading them into the vast crowded hall. 'Almost every superhero on the planet is probably in this building somewhere.'

Stan looked around. Most people had come dressed in superhero costumes, so it was hard to tell which were actually famous. He'd been looking forward to this trip for weeks. There were stalls selling books, posters, silk capes, masks, signed photos and deadly hypno-rings for £1.99. He picked up a packet from a nearby stall and read the label.

'Hey, check out this bubblegum,' he said, showing Minnie.

'Bionic?' said Minnie. 'It's probably as bionic as your brain.'

'Are you buying that or not?' demanded the stallholder – a man wearing a pair of ears that lit up like fairy lights.

'How much is it?' asked Stan.

'One ninety-five.'

'For a packet of bubblegum?' said Minnie.

'It's bionic, love,' said the man. 'Can't you read?'

Stan handed over the money. He still had some left, which he was saving to get a copy of Captain Courageous's latest book: **BORN SUPER!** Ever since Stan was old enough to wear a cape he'd idolised Captain Courageous and dreamed of meeting him.

Now here he was, a pupil at Mighty High School, training to join the ranks of tomorrow's superheroes. Soon after he had started at Mighty High, he'd made firm friends with Miles, Minnie and Pudding the Wonderdog. Together they'd formed **the Invincibles**, probably the greatest superhero gang in their class (and certainly the only one).

Stan pointed to a life-sized picture of a superhero with his fist raised to the sky.

'**Wow!** He's actually here,' he cried. 'Captain Courageous!'

The sign said his idol would be signing books in the main hall at two o'clock. 'What are we waiting for?' asked Minnie. 'Let's go!'

Miles looked around anxiously. 'Um ... actually, I need the toilet.'

They walked past rows of souvenir stalls to reach the main hall. Stan stared in disbelief.

'You're kidding me!' he groaned. The queue snaked twice round the hall and back down the corridor.

'We'll have to wait *hours* to meet him,' said Minnie.

'But it's Captain Courageous, we can't give up now,' argued Stan.

'Sorry, but I really *really* need the toilet,' said Miles, jiggling around.

'Hurry up, then,' sighed Minnie. 'We'll be in the queue.'

Miles headed off down the corridor as Stan rubbed his ear. 'You're doing it again,' said Minnie.

'What?'

'That thing you always do with your ears.'

Stan shrugged. 'I can't help it, they started itching just now.'

Ever since he was little his ears had warned him when something bad was about to happen. Sometimes it only turned out to be Brussels sprouts for dinner, but occasionally it was a lot worse. It had earned him the nickname **DANGERBOY**.

Minnie laughed. 'This place is crawling with superheroes. What could possibly go wrong?' she said.

Meanwhile, Miles had finally located the boys' toilets. He came out of a cubicle and went to a basin to wash his hands.

Suddenly the walls shook as if an elephant had sat down, and brilliant white light flooded the room. Miles screwed up his eyes, holding on to the basin for support. Was it an earthquake? What was happening? Eventually the floor stopped shaking. Going to the window, he stood on tiptoe and peered out. The car park looked like any normal car park, with rows of cars, a ticket machine, half a dozen coaches and a spaceship parked under a lamp post.

A SPACESHIP?

Where in Zog's name did that come from? thought Miles. He looked around, half expecting to see police cars arrive with their sirens wailing. Nothing happened. He wondered if he ought to fetch someone – a teacher, or maybe the car park attendant?

But it wasn't the kind of thing that anyone would believe – a spaceship parked outside the leisure centre.

In any case Miles had always wanted to see a flying saucer, and this was his chance.

Standing on one of the toilet seats, Miles managed to heave himself up to a window ledge and wriggle out. The spaceship sat steaming in the sunlight. It was enormous. Miles crept closer.

ZWOOBB!

Suddenly a door in the craft slid open. Miles ducked behind a car just in time to see two strange creatures emerge. *Aliens!* Miles knew they were aliens by their green skin and their weird taste in clothes – basically, they weren't wearing any. They had large melon-shaped heads and sticky suckers in place of hands and feet. They oozed down the ramp with a sound like fish slithering down a wall.

The aliens looked about them and caught
sight of a giant billboard. It showed Captain
Courageous advertising Titan Hair Gel for
Men. They stared at it, talking in weird high
voices. Obviously Miles couldn't understand a
word, as he didn't speak Alien.

KEEP YOUR HAIR SUPER
like CAPTAIN
COURAGEOUS
with TITAN
HAIR GEL
TITAN
HAIR GEL
OOH! CAPTAIN K-JUICE
NOG!
YEG!
NOG BIMSTINKLE
WHO YOU CALLING BIMSTINKLE?

Miles raised his head above the car bonnet, trying to work out what they were doing. He wished Stan and Minnie were here to see this. Aliens from another planet! They would never believe him in a million years. Unless ...

Miles felt in his pocket for the new mobile phone he'd got for Christmas. So far he'd only received three text messages, which were all

from his mum – but the phone had a built-in camera. If he could just get near enough he could take a picture.

He crept forward to the next row of cars. The aliens were so close he could see the greens of their eyes. Slowly, he raised his head, holding the mobile phone high in the air. Trying to stop his arm trembling he took a picture ...

Uh-oh, he should have remembered the camera phone made a noise. Nine green eyes whipped round and fastened on him.

'EARTHLIG!' hissed the aliens. Miles thought of making a run for it, but when people did that in films they usually got zapped before they got far. Besides, maybe the aliens were friendly? Miles raised his hands above his head in surrender.

'It's OK!' he said. 'I'm not going to hurt you. I, er … I come in peace!'

It was hard to tell if the aliens understood.

Captain K-Juice?' said the smaller one, pointing to Miles.

'Neg, dum-dum. Him weaklig.'

Miles held out his mobile phone.

'I only wanted to take your picture,' he explained. 'You know – picture? I can show you if you like?'

The aliens oozed towards him with a sucking, squelchy noise. Possibly they wanted to take a selfie to show their alien chums back home?

Miles wasn't exactly sure how to greet aliens, so he nodded, smiled and bowed at the same time. One of the aliens stuck out his tongue, which was long, green and disgustingly sticky. Suddenly it snaked out and attached itself to Miles's forehead.

The next moment his feet left the ground and he was flying through the air. He hit the gravel and was dragged across the car park towards the spaceship.

'Wait! Let's talk ...' he pleaded as he was hauled up the ramp. The door of the spaceship yawned open.

The next moment it slid shut with a hiss and Miles found himself in utter darkness. He hoped this was the alien way of inviting you round for supper.

Chapter 2

Miles Ahead

Stan, Minnie and Pudding waited to get on the coach. They'd wasted half the morning queuing to meet Captain Courageous, only to be told the books had sold out and their idol had left for a chat show.

Miss Marbles counted the class as they got on.

'Twenty-five, twenty-six, twenty-seven … Someone's missing,' she said. 'Who is not here? Hands up!'

Tank raised his hand. 'I'm not, miss,' he said.

'Don't be stupid, Tank,' said Miss Marbles. 'This is a serious matter. Who isn't back?'

Stan looked up. 'I think it's Miles, miss. We lost him earlier.'

'Lost him? How did you lose him?' asked the head teacher.

'Well, he went to the toilet and never came back,' explained Stan.

He didn't think anyone could get lost going to the toilet, but with Miles nothing would surprise him. His head was so stuffed with useless information there was no room for common sense.

Miles was the only person he knew who had 'right' and 'left' written on the soles of his shoes so he wouldn't put them on the wrong feet.

Stan rubbed his ear. There was the tingling feeling again, warning him that something was wrong. What if Miles had landed himself in some kind of trouble or locked himself in a toilet and couldn't get out? Pudding the Wonderdog suddenly leapt on to a seat and barked excitedly.

'Look, there he is!' cried Minnie, pointing.

Everyone rushed to the window to look.
Miles was walking away from them down
the road.

Actually, he was walking *IN* the road.
Drivers honked their horns and swerved to
avoid him as he wandered through the traffic
like a sleepwalker.

'MILES! Get back here this minute!' shouted Miss Marbles, leaning out of the coach. Miles stopped in his tracks and turned his head. He changed direction, cutting across two lanes of traffic.

Back on the coach, Miss Marbles gave Miles a long lecture about road safety. Usually when Miles was in trouble he turned red as a beetroot, but this time he stared blankly at the head teacher as if she were speaking Ancient Greek. Eventually Miss Marbles told him to go and sit down.

Miles came down the aisle and would have
walked straight past Stan if he hadn't grabbed
him by the arm.

'Hey, Brainbox, I saved you a seat,'
said Stan.

Miles blinked at him through his round
glasses. 'Seat?' he repeated.

'Yes, a seat, Dumbo. Sit down,' said Stan.

Miss Marbles was watching them impatiently, wanting to set off. Stan pulled Miles down into the seat beside him.

'How do you do-do?' asked Miles, offering his hand.

'What?'

'Me Miles, peas to meet you,' said Miles.

'What are you on about?' sighed Stan. 'And where have you *been* all this time?'

'Where have *you* beans?' replied Miles.

'Right here, waiting for YOU,' said Stan. 'We were starting to get worried.'

The coach set off. Miles stared out of the window at the passing cars, making little beeping noises to himself. Minnie leaned forward from the seat behind.

'What's up with him?' she whispered.

'Don't ask me; his brain's overheated,' said Stan. 'Maybe he walked into a door or something.'

While Miles continued beeping at cars, Stan pulled out the packet of bubblegum he'd bought earlier. He wondered how bionic bubblegum was different to any other kind, but there was nothing on the packet except a warning not to chew indoors. The coach wasn't exactly indoors, thought Stan. Checking that Miss Marbles wasn't looking, he tore open the packet. Inside were four foil-wrapped sticks of gum.

'Anyone want to try some bionic gum?' asked Stan, lowering his voice.

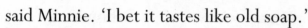

'No, thanks,' said Minnie. 'I bet it tastes like old soap.'

Stan didn't have a chance to find out because Miles grabbed the packet from his hand.

Before Stan
could stop him
he crammed
two sticks of
bubblegum
into his
mouth.
'Hey!' cried
Stan. 'You're meant
to take off the paper!'

'Gubblebum,'
said Miles, putting
out his tongue,
which had
turned blue.

'It's
supposed to
be bionic,'
said Stan. 'You
have to chew it.'

'GUBBLE, GUBBLEBUM,'

replied Miles, his jaw working as he chewed.

'Told you it was a waste of money,' sighed Minnie. 'Not even a tiny bubble.'

'He's not doing it right,' said Stan. 'Try blowing, Miles, like this.' He demonstrated, making an 'O' shape with his lips. Miles copied.

A small blue bubble bloomed from his mouth and promptly popped, making him jump.

'Not so fast,' said Stan. 'Do it slowly.'

Miles tried again. This time he got the hang of it and the bubble started to grow before their eyes. It swelled to the size of a tennis ball. That would have been impressive but it didn't stop there. The bubble kept inflating like a giant blue balloon. Miles had gone cross-eyed with the effort and his glasses had steamed up.

'Amazing!' said Stan. 'I told you it was bionic!'

Minnie was keeping her eye on Miss Marbles. They weren't allowed sweets on the coach.

'OK, you win, but shouldn't you get him to stop?' she asked.

Miles wasn't listening. The bionic bubble kept growing, swelling at an alarming rate. Stan's classmates had noticed and were nudging each other, turning round in their seats to look.

'Enough now, Miles,' said Stan. 'You'll get us in trouble.'

But the bionic bubblegum wasn't finished. The bubble was starting to rise and Miles was going with it, floating out of his seat.

'Quick, Stan, grab him,' hissed Minnie.

Stan tried but it was no use. Miles kept
rising till he was spreadeagled on the ceiling
like an astronaut in zero gravity. Meanwhile,
the bionic bubble was still getting bigger. Stan
was just wondering how Miles would get
down when …

The bubble popped, splattering Miles's startled face with gummy goo. He fell off the ceiling, landing on top of them in a tangle of arms and legs.

Stan looked up to see Miss Marbles standing over them, wearing a cross expression.

'Really!' she said. 'I have told you before not to chew gum on the coach! I hope that's a lesson to you, Miles.'

Miles climbed off Minnie and wiped a glob of sticky blue goo from his hair.

'Gubblebum,' he said, putting it in his mouth. Back in their seats, Minnie and Stan looked worried. Miles was certainly behaving strangely.

First he'd wandered off down the middle of a busy road, then he'd talked gibberish and got stuck to the roof of the coach. Stan hoped he wasn't planning anything else before they got back to school.

'Are you OK, Miles?' he asked.

'Hokay,' replied Miles. 'Captain K-Juice.' He pressed his face to the window again.

Miss Marbles clapped her hands to get their attention.

'Now, while we're all here I'd like to go over one or two things,' she said. 'As I'm sure you're all aware, this Friday you'll be taking your Heroes.'

The class looked at her blankly.

'Your **HEROES**,' said the head teacher. 'Your **FiRST-YEAR EXAMS**.'

'What exams?' asked Stan, voicing the question on everyone's lips. It was only the summer term – their third at Mighty High – and nobody had mentioned exams.

Miss Marbles frowned and took off her glasses.

'Didn't you get a letter home about this?' she asked. 'No? Well anyway, all pupils must sit their Heroes in their first year. You need to pass these exams if you wish to remain at Mighty High.'

Stan felt his stomach flip over. Exams? He was hopeless at exams! It was Monday now, so if the exams were on Friday they only had a few days to prepare for them!

One thing he'd learned about Mighty High was that nothing was ever predictable. Exams could mean anything at all – from reciting your times tables to facing killer robots.

When Stan had come for his interview, Miss Marbles had invited him to run head first into a brick wall. Who knew what HEROES might involve?

Minnie had her hand in the air.

'But what kind of exams, miss?' she asked. 'Will it be answering questions?'

'Naturally, questions, among other things,' said Miss Marbles, vaguely. 'But don't look so worried. I'm sure that you'll pass with flying colours – most of you. Of course, there is always a practical because we need to test how your superpowers are developing. And speaking of that, please remember your crash helmets tomorrow. Professor Bird will be taking your first lesson.'

Stan swallowed hard. Professor Bird's lessons were the subject of wild rumours around the school. Some people claimed that his methods were effective, while others whispered that he was nutty as a fruitcake. The only thing everyone agreed on was the subject Professor Bird taught: flying.

DON'T BE GOOD, BE SUPER.

PROPERTY OF MIGHTY HIGH SCHOOL

The Pocket Guide for Superheroes

Everything you need to know to save the world.

3

EXAMS

Is there any other word that strikes such terror into the human heart?

Most superheroes would rather eat their own earwax than have to sit an exam.

Let's face facts. To pass exams, you need to be one of three things:

a) Brainy

b) Lucky

c) Extremely sneaky

If, like me, you don't happen to be a or b), then sneakiness is your best chance.

SUPER WAYS TO PASS EXAMS

1. X- RAY VISION

With X-ray vision, you need never be stuck for an answer.

2. TIME TRAVEL

Set your time-travel device to the near future when the papers are handed back. Copy out the answers and return to begin your exam. Simples.

3. MIND MELDING

Gain access to the mind of the annoying nerd sitting next to you.

↑ Nerd

Note: if they're thinking about chocolate, this doesn't work so well.

4. SUPER BREATH

If all else fails, you can always upset that pile of completed test papers. It's so easy to pick up the wrong one by mistake.

Finally, remember that passing exams is actually the easy part. Getting through the practical, now that's the bit that should keep you awake at night.

Chapter 4

Flying Lessons

Professor Bird was wearing a long
black gown, leather gloves and a
pair of ancient flying goggles on
his head. He rubbed his hands
together.

'Excellent!' he said. 'Clearish
sky, slight breeze, good visibility –
a perfect day for flying.'

Stan squinted up at the sky, which
seemed to be the usual cloudy grey.

He wondered how much it would have to rain before the lesson would be cancelled.

The truth was he'd been dreading this moment ever since Miss Marbles had told them they were to have their first flying lesson. The class had gathered on the lawn beside the outdoor swimming pool, which looked like it hadn't been used since Queen Victoria was on the throne. These days the pool was empty, with spidery cracks in the cement floor and weeds sprouting like mushrooms.

'So,' said Professor Bird. 'Hands up, who has always wanted to fly?'

Every hand in the class shot up, including Stan's.

All the same, he suspected that if he could fly he probably would have discovered it by now. He'd spent countless hours jumping off his bed but he'd never flown once or even hovered a little. To be honest, the thought of

leaping from the edge of a skyscraper made him
feel weak at the knees.

'Of course, flying isn't something you will
master in a few short lessons,' Professor Bird
was saying. 'It will take courage, skill and blind
faith in the impossible. So to begin with, I want
you to become more confident by gaining some
practice.'

Stan raised his hand. 'But, sir, what if we've never flown before?' he asked.

The Professor snorted. 'Of course you've never flown before. That's why we are here!'

'Yes, but I mean, what if we, um … can't?' asked Stan.

'*Can't?*' repeated the Professor. 'Do you think anyone became a fearless superhero by saying "*Can't*"?'

'Well, no,' mumbled Stan.

'*No* – and besides, if you never try, you'll never find out, will you?' demanded Professor Bird.

Stan shook his head, wishing the teacher would pick on someone else. He glanced at the rest of the class, most of whom looked equally nervous. Minnie was stroking Pudding's head as if she wanted to wear a hole in it. Tank's small brain was working overtime, trying to think of a way out of this. Norris Trimble was twisting his hanky into knots. Only Miles stared up at the sky and didn't seem to be paying attention.

Stan wondered what the pool was for – if the Professor wanted them to swim lengths, it would be tricky without water. He guessed that they'd find out soon enough.

'So who can tell me the first rule of flying?' asked Professor Bird.

'Um … don't look down?' suggested Minnie.

'NO, the first rule of flying is "Let go",' said the Professor. 'Let go of your fears, your logical mind. Imagine you are light as a feather floating on air.'

Stan tried to imagine it but could only think of himself falling like a stone. His ears had begun to tingle, which made him more nervous.

'So, as it's your first flying lesson, we'll start with something easy,' said Professor Bird. 'Jumping off the *high-*diving board.'

Stan looked up. Was the Professor out of his mind? 'But, sir, there's no water in the pool,' he pointed out.

'Well spotted,' said Professor Bird. 'But the idea is to fly, not to dive in head first. If it makes you feel better, we'll have someone standing below to catch you.'

The Professor asked for volunteers and Tank's hand shot up immediately. He was stationed in the pool with two others to hold a blanket and catch children as they plummeted to earth. He smirked at Stan, happy to have escaped the high-diving board.

Everyone else was told to line up by the steps. There was a mad scramble to avoid being first in the line. Stan found himself shoved to the front, with only Norris Trimble ahead of him. He gazed at the three flights of metal steps. It was obviously called the high-diving board for a reason. His ears were now on red alert.

'Isn't it a bit dangerous, sir?' gulped Norris.

'Nonsense!' said Professor Bird. 'I've taught this lesson for years and no one's died yet. Relax! Let go! Enjoy yourself!'

Stan turned and caught Minnie's eye. They'd been asked to do some crazy things at Mighty High,

but diving into an empty swimming pool beat just about everything. He wished he were wearing rocket boots or maybe some kind of parachute cape that would open up.

Slowly he began to climb the steps behind the trembling Norris. Every footstep echoed with a dull clang.

Reaching the top, Stan paused to get his

breath back and looked down. This was a bad mistake. The ground was way below. A wave of dizziness swept over him and he grabbed hold of the handrail to steady himself.

'First one, then,' cried the Professor. 'We haven't got all day!'

Norris gulped and inched out on to the diving board. Suddenly he turned round, clapped a hand over his mouth and bolted past Stan.

There was the sound of someone being sick from a great height. Professor Bird shook his head and turned his attention to Stan.

'STEP OUT, NEXT BOY!'

he shouted. 'Let go! Imagine you're a great eagle!'

Stan felt more like a great-grandmother. He remembered now why he was scared of heights – they were downright dangerous. He put one foot on the diving board, which creaked under his weight. Far below he could see Tank and the others holding the blanket, which looked smaller than a paper hanky.

What if I can't fly? What if they don't catch me? thought Stan. At that moment, the diving board began to wobble and shake alarmingly. Stan turned to see Miles behind him, bouncing up and down like an overexcited kangaroo.

'Miles, DON'T!' shouted Stan, struggling to keep his balance.

'BOINGY BOINGY!' cried Miles.

'No, *not* boingy boingy,' said Stan. 'You'll make us … ARGHHHHH!'

Too late, he slipped from the board and tumbled backwards through the air.

'Let go! FLY!' yelled Professor Bird. Stan flapped his arms. The wind roared in his ears as he felt the ground rushing towards him. The next moment he crash-landed on something big and soft …

Luckily it was Tank, who was holding the blanket.

OOOF!

'Get off, you great numpty!' roared Tank. Stan clambered off him, surprised to find that nothing seemed to be hurt besides Tank's feelings. It was lucky he was so well padded.

'MILES!' It was Minnie who screamed.

Stan looked up to see Miles perched precariously on the end of the high-diving board. He was bouncing on his toes with his arms raised as if preparing for a double somersault. Without anyone holding the blanket, he would splat like a tomato.

'Miles, wait … !' yelled Stan, but it was no use.

Miles looked into the sky as if expecting something, then dived through the air, hurtling towards them.

Stan watched in astonishment as Miles swooped over their heads like a low-flying jet. He performed a neat loop-the-loop, coming gently to rest beside the swimming pool. He made it all look as simple and normal as scratching his bottom.

'Whoa! That was insane!' cried Stan. Miles nodded. 'Captain K-Juice,' he said, sounding a little disappointed.

The rest of the class came running over to congratulate him, whooping and cheering.

'Bravo! Superb!' cried Professor Bird, arriving out of breath. 'I knew it. Sooner or later I knew someone would do it!'

Stan looked at him open-mouthed. 'You mean that's the first time anyone's actually flown?' he asked.

'Of course, there's always a first time!' beamed the Professor. 'Now then, who wants to go next?'

But if that's the REAL Miles, then who is the Miles at school with Stan and Minnie?

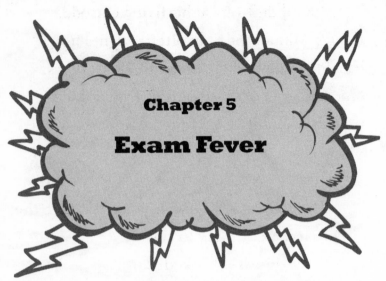

Chapter 5

Exam Fever

Back at Mighty High, the rest of the week raced by, with normal lessons interrupted by Professor Bird's flying classes. The Professor introduced a trampoline, but the success rate remained at a steady zero. (Other than Miles.)

AAAAARRGH

Miles didn't repeat his flying episode, though Minnie and Stan often caught him hanging around by the third-floor windows. Once he even climbed on to the gym-block roof. It was as if he was expecting someone to show up.

All too soon, Friday came round – the day of the dreaded exams. The Invincibles sat in the old library, attempting to revise.

'What time is it?' asked Stan.

Minnie sighed. 'Three minutes since the last time you asked,' she said. 'Stop fidgeting!

You don't see Pudding getting nervous.'

'He's a dog!' said Stan. 'He doesn't have to take exams.'

'I'm sure it will all be fine,' said Minnie.

'But what if it isn't?' asked Stan. 'What if I look at the exam paper and my mind goes completely blank?'

Exams had never been Stan's strong point. He'd once scored minus two in a maths test.

When he started at Mighty High, he'd hoped that exams would be a thing of the past, but apparently not even superheroes could escape them. Worst of all, failure meant having to leave school. Stan's dream of becoming a real superhero would be over. He'd have to hand back his cape and return to being ordinary Stanley Button. No more **DANGERBOY** – no more missions with the Invincibles.

The most dangerous part of his day would be eating school dinners.

Minnie was flicking through the pages of their school textbook, *The Pocket Guide for Superheroes*. At the back of the book was a section with multiple-choice questions.

'OK, ask me something,' said Stan.

'Why can't you sit still?' asked Minnie.

'No, I mean a test question.'

'OK, what do all supervillains want?' asked Minnie.

a) To be popular

b) To rule the world

c) Free ice cream for life

'That's easy – to rule the world,' answered Stan. He hoped all the questions were as simple as this.

'Correct,' said Minnie. 'See, it's not so difficult. Your go, Miles. Name three uses for a pair of tights.'

Miles was trying to get rid of a piece of paper, which seemed to be stuck like glue to his fingers.

'Miles! Are you even listening?' demanded Minnie.

Miles looked at her blankly.

'Captain K-Juice,' he mumbled.

Minnie rolled her eyes. Since the school trip at the start of the week it had been impossible to get any sense out of him. He wandered around in a dream, mumbling to himself or staring at the sky. Mostly he repeated the name '**Captain K-Juice**' and opened cupboard doors as if someone might be hiding inside.

Minnie watched him cross to the library window. 'Don't you think he's been acting weird?' she sighed.

'You mean even weirder than usual?' asked Stan.

'Yes! It's like he's in a world of his own,' replied Minnie.

Stan nodded. Miles had always been a little unusual; he knew answers to questions that Stan didn't even know existed. But recently he seemed like a complete stranger. Flying, for instance – where had he picked that up?

'Maybe it's the exams,' Stan suggested. 'They do funny things to people.'

Minnie shook her head. 'It started before that,' she said. 'Remember at the **Superhero Fan Convention?** He disappeared, then next thing he's wandering off down the middle of the road!'

'Shh!' whispered Stan. 'He'll hear you.'

'I doubt it,' said Minnie. 'And what about the exams? The way he's going on, he could fail completely.'

'Oh, come on,' said Stan. 'Miles is the biggest brainiac in the class.'

'Is he?' asked Minnie. 'Look at him.'

Miles had his nose pressed against the window and seemed to be licking it. Suddenly he gave a gasp and banged his hands on the glass.

Out on the road a number 9 bus was passing. A giant poster on the side carried the slogan: **TITAN HAIR GEL FOR REAL MEN** with the handsome face of Captain Courageous next to it.

'**Captain K-Juice!**' yelled Miles, pointing at the bus.

Stan rolled his eyes. 'Relax, it's just an advert,' he said. 'Come and sit down.'

But Miles didn't seem to hear. He pressed against the window, gripping the handle. Suddenly it opened, flipping over and catapulting him outside.

They rushed over. Fortunately the library was only one floor up, so Miles had landed safely. He was back on his feet, chasing the bus as it sped down the road.

'Where are you going?' Stan shouted. 'Come back!'

But Miles kept running down the drive and out of the school gates. Pudding barked, keen to join the game.

'Come on,' said Minnie. 'We've got to get him back.'

'NOW?' said Stan. 'But what about the exams?'

'If we hurry we'll be back in time,' said Minnie, glancing at her watch.

They had less than half an hour. Stan climbed out of the window and jumped down. Even if they didn't miss the exams they'd probably be expelled for bunking off school. If he caught up with Miles he was going to strangle him.

Chapter 6

Don't Look Down

They chased Miles down the road. He was tearing along at high speed, bumping into people with his eyes fixed on the bus. Stan wondered what he planned to do if he ever caught it. What was this mad obsession with Captain Courageous? In the past he'd never mentioned the name. Now a picture on a bus sent him crazy.

Finally the bus turned a corner and they lost sight of it. Stan bent over, out of breath.

They had
come out into a
large open square.
Children played
around a fountain and
a few people sat on
benches, enjoying the
afternoon sun. Stan
looked around for Miles.

'This is hopeless,' he said, shaking his
head. If they didn't get back soon they would
certainly miss the exam. It was at times like
this he wished his superpower was travelling
at the speed of light rather than oversensitive
ears. Talking of which, they were tingling
now.

Minnie pointed to a billboard at the far
end of the square. Miles was scaling it like a fly
crawling up a wall. There seemed to be no end
to the surprising things he could do.

'What's he up to now?' groaned Stan.

'Miles! Get down! You'll break your neck!' shouted Minnie.

The billboard was the size of a cinema screen but Miles was reaching the top. He hauled himself up, then sat with his legs dangling either side. His stunt had started to draw a crowd. Stan, Minnie and Pudding were attracting a few odd looks too. They'd forgotten they were wearing their capes and superhero costumes.

'Is it fancy dress?' asked an old lady.

'DON'T MOVE, MILES, WE'RE COMING!' shouted Minnie.

'We are?' said Stan.

'Of course, we can't just leave him,' said Minnie. 'If Miles can do it, so can we.'

Stan looked up at the enormous billboard. After his experience with the high-diving board, he preferred to keep his feet on solid ground.

'I'm not good with heights,' he said. 'You go.'

'ME?' said Minnie.

'Yes, you want to rescue him.'

Stan couldn't see how he was meant to climb a billboard anyway. He'd need ropes, or a ladder – or better still, elastic arms like

RUBBER MAN.

Minnie put her head in her hands.
Apparently sitting on top of a giant billboard
wasn't dangerous enough for Miles; now he
wanted to practise his tightrope walking. He
rose slowly to his feet with his arms waving in
the air.

'The idiot! He'll kill himself,' moaned
Minnie. 'Do something!'

Stan cupped his hands to his mouth. **'BE
CAREFUL, MILES!'** he yelled.

'"Be careful"?' said Minnie. 'Is that it?'

'It's good advice,' said Stan. 'My mum says
it all the time.'

In any case, Miles wasn't paying attention. He had one foot on the billboard and the other wobbling in mid-air. Stan couldn't bear to watch. Miles swayed for a moment, flapped his arms wildly, then lost his balance and fell.

BIG ADVERTISING CO. LTD

People screamed. Stan hoped that Miles remembered he could fly. But he needn't have worried because suddenly a scarlet figure zoomed out of the sky and plucked Miles from the air.

'Captain Courageous!' gasped Minnie as the famous superhero landed neatly.

Stan had no idea where he'd come from but he was exactly as he appeared on TV: broad shoulders, square jaw and hair that looked like a shampoo advert.

'Stand back, people!' he ordered. 'Give the kid some air!'

He set Miles's feet on the ground.

'Captain K-Juice!' said Miles, correctly for once.

'That's right, buddy, you're safe now, you can let go of me,' said his rescuer.

But Miles didn't loosen his grip. Having found Captain Courageous at long last, he wasn't letting go of him that quickly.

'Um, anyone know this kid?' asked Captain Courageous.

'We do,' said Stan, stepping forward. 'He's with us.'

'We're superheroes too,' added Minnie.

Captain Courageous looked them up and down. 'Right,' he said. 'Aren't you a bit young?'

'We're still in training,' explained Stan, loweing his voice. 'We go to Mighty High. It's like a secret school for superheroes of the future.'

'You don't say?' Captain Courageous was looking at them as if they were barking mad. It was probably because Pudding was wearing a blue cape, which you didn't see on a dog every day.

The Captain shook Stan's hand firmly. 'Well, nice meeting you guys. I better be going,' he said. 'Keep up the good work.'

He frowned at Miles, who was still hanging round his neck like a scarf.

'Let go now, buddy,' he said.

'**Captain K-Juice,**' repeated Miles.

Stan wasn't sure how it happened, but a
second later the two of them launched into
the air.

At first Stan thought Captain Courageous was taking Miles – but it seemed to be the other way round. Miles had one arm round the Captain's neck and was dragging him backwards.

'Hey! What in Zog's name … ?' croaked the superhero.

Stan watched in amazement as they swooped over buildings and vanished out of sight.

'What just happened?' asked Stan.

'I'm not sure,' said Minnie. 'Did Miles *kidnap* Captain Courageous?'

Stan frowned. 'It sort of looked that way.'

'But why would he do that?' asked Minnie.

Stan had no idea – but then nothing about Miles made sense any more. Up until a few days ago they had no idea he could fly. He looked at his watch.

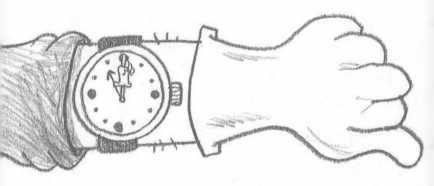

'The exam!' he groaned. 'It starts in five minutes!'

Minnie shook her head. 'Can't be helped,' she said.

'What do you mean, can't be helped?' cried Stan. 'If we don't pass our Heroes we'll be thrown out! We're finished!'

'It's a chance we'll have to take,' said Minnie. 'What's the first duty of a superhero?'

Stan rolled his eyes. 'Don't ask me! Is this a test question?'

'No, our first duty is to help anyone who's in danger,' said Minnie. 'And Miles needs us – or Captain Courageous does – one of the two. Either way, something's definitely not right. How are your ears?'

'Burning up,' admitted Stan, rubbing them.

'Just as I thought,' said Minnie. 'Come on, we've got to find them before it's too late.'

Chapter 7

Sticky Situation

'Why would they come here?' Stan asked.

They'd arrived at the leisure centre, where, a few days ago, the Superhero Fan Convention had taken place. It was Pudding who'd led them here because Minnie insisted the wonderdog had picked up the scent. However, the leisure centre looked deserted. There was nothing in the car park except one or two cars, a row of wheelie bins and a silver spaceship, hovering above the ground.

Stan stared as the craft landed smoothly on
the gravel. 'Is that what I think it is?' he asked.

'Well, it's not a burger van,' said Minnie.

'Maybe it's a fake or something?'

But the spaceship looked real enough.
Steam rose from the gleaming dome as if it had
just been through a car wash. Lights winked on
and off and a low hum filled the air.

'What now?' whispered Stan. 'Do we knock on the door?'

'**SHHHH!** Someone's coming,' hissed Minnie. They ducked down behind a row of wheelie bins, just in time to see two people cross the car park. One was Miles, who had Captain Courageous gripped by the arm.

'Look, I don't want to be rude but ... **HOLY UNDERPANTS!**' cried the

Captain, catching sight of the spaceship for the first time.

A door in the craft slid open with a hiss and a ramp was lowered. Four strange creatures emerged from the ship and slithered down the ramp. They had green skin, three eyes and heads the shape of light bulbs. They also seemed to have forgotten to get dressed that morning.

'Aliens!' gasped Stan. His ears were telling him to run, but it was too late now. Pudding let out a frightened whimper and ducked behind Minnie.

The aliens crowded round Captain Courageous, reaching out to touch his clothes. **'AHHH! Captain K-Juice!'** they burbled.

Their hero nodded and swept back his mane of blond hair. He was used to this sort of star-struck reaction from fans.

'What's up, guys?' he said. 'Nice costumes. So what is this, some sort of charity thing?'

'Captain K-Juice!' burbled one of the aliens, reaching up to poke him in the eye.

'OUCH! Yup, that's me,' said Courageous. 'Is there something I can do for you?'

The alien who seemed to be the leader held out one of the sticky suckers that served as hands. All the others copied him.

'**Name,**' he said. '**Captain K-Juice.**'

'Right, Captain Courageous, that's my name,' said the superhero.

'**Write name. Write!**' The alien made a squiggling action using one of his suckers.

'Oh, you want an *autograph*?' said Captain Courageous, finally getting it. 'No problem! Anyone got a pen?'

Stan and Minnie watched, mystified, as the superhero signed his name on a dozen alien suckers. (One of them wanted his head autographed.) Captain Courageous still seemed to think he was meeting a group of fans dressed in funny green costumes.

When it was done, the aliens compared their autographs, burbling excitedly.

'So, it was great to meet you guys,' said Captain Courageous. 'I love the whole alien thing with the masks and spaceship. But, you know, got to fly now.'

'FLYNOW?' repeated the alien commander.

'Yes, fly, you know, things to do, people to save,' smiled Captain Courageous. The aliens didn't smile back, though it was hard to tell, as only their eyes moved.

'Well, be seeing you!' Courageous raised one arm in the air and took off – or at least he would have done, if a sticky hand hadn't wrapped around his foot like ivy and pulled him back to earth.

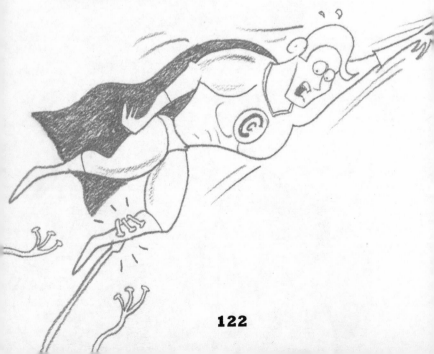

'Hey, cut that out … !' protested Captain Courageous as he was dragged towards the spaceship.

'Uh-oh. Shouldn't we do something?' whispered Minnie.

Stan looked at her. 'It's Captain Courageous. Any moment now he'll escape and flatten the lot of them –

They waited for the Captain to demonstrate his super-strength, but he seemed too busy yelling at the top of his voice. 'HEEEELP! SOMEBODY!' he wailed.

The alien leader barked an order and the door slid shut.

Minnie turned to Stan and raised her eyebrows. 'So, you were saying?'

DON'T BE GOOD, BE SUPER.

PROPERTY OF MIGHTY HIGH SCHOOL

The Pocket Guide for Superheroes

Everything you need to know to save the world.

3

ALIENS

Aliens: sooner or later we all run into them. If your ambition is to become a superhero, be prepared to face enemies in all shapes and sizes. The secret is to work out who – or what – you're dealing with. Supervillains are usually predictabl creatures with one ambition: world domination.

Aliens are more complicated and don't have much time for small talk before they vaporise you. Be alert – aliens will often adopt cunning disguises in order to fool you.

a)

b)

c)

d)

If you believe you could be dealing with an alien, try this simple test: get close enough to SMELL them. Do they smell of ...
a) Sweat
b) Cheese and onion crisps
c) Nothing

SNIFF

If the answer is c), they are probably an **ALIEN**. Either that or you have a cold and probably shouldn't be sniffing people.

Chapter 9

Double Trouble

Stan and Minnie crouched behind the wheelie bins, trying to think of a plan. Were they too late? If the spaceship launched into the sky then they might never see Miles again – or Captain Courageous, for that matter. While Stan was asking these questions, the door of the spacecraft slid open again and two figures fell out, tumbling down the ramp. They seemed to be wrestling.

Minnie jumped up. 'It's Miles!' she cried.

'Which one? They're both Miles!' said
Stan.

They stared in disbelief. Two Miles seemed
to be having a fight with themselves. They each
had the same brown hair, short legs and thick
round glasses. The only difference was that one
Miles seemed to be a lot better at fighting than
the other. He flung his double to the ground
and jumped on top of him.

'Don't just stand there, help him!' cried Minnie.

'Which one?' said Stan.

It was impossible to tell – and they could easily rescue the wrong one.

'Pudding – he'll know!' said Minnie. 'Dogs recognise people by their smell.'

She turned to Pudding, who had looked up at hearing his name.

'Pud-Pud's, where's Miles? Find him, boy!' said Minnie, pointing.

Pudding barked and bounded away across the car park. By now the stronger Miles was sitting on top of his opponent, pulling him by the ears.

Pudding bent down and licked the Miles on the ground.

'That sounds like Miles all right,' said
Minnie. 'Come on!'

They raced forward and dragged the
imposter Miles off. Stan and Minnie took a
hand each and flung him backwards into the
wheelie bins, which toppled over, burying him
under a pile of rubbish.

The real Miles got to his knees, breathing heavily.

'What took you so long?' he grumbled, holding his sore ears.

'How were we to know you needed help?' asked Minnie. 'We thought HE was you.'

She pointed to the dazed alien lying in the rubbish with a banana skin on his head.

'He's an alien, for heaven's sake,' said Miles. 'He's way uglier than me!'

'Never mind that now,' said Stan. 'They've still got Captain Courageous!'

'STOP EARTHLIGS!'

A loud metallic voice made them whirl round.

They turned to see the alien commander at the door of his spaceship, flanked by his underlings. Captain Courageous stood beside him with a deadly ray gun pointed at his head.

'**Resistance is useless!**' said the alien commander. '**Surrender or Captain K-Juice dries.**'

'He dries?' repeated Stan. 'When did he get wet?'

'I think he means "dies",' muttered Captain Courageous.

They had little choice but to obey. Stan raised his arms in the air. As Minnie obeyed, she slid her frisbee from her belt. Stan's eyes widened. What was she playing at?

In a split second Captain Courageous had broken free and two of his guards lay sprawled on the ground. He somersaulted down the ramp and landed in front of the Invincibles.

'Impressive, huh?' he said. 'Now let's see what these green goons are made of. I'm guessing you guys have some kind of superpowers?'

'Sort of,' replied Stan. 'My ears detect danger.'

'And I'm Frisbee Girl,' said Minnie.

'And I, er … know a lot of stuff,' said Miles.

'Right, not quite what I had in mind,' said Captain Courageous. 'But stick with me and you'll be … Uhh, where did they go?'

The aliens had retreated into their spaceship with the door closing behind them. The next moment the craft hummed into life and took off with a whoosh of booster rockets.

'HA! Scaredy-cats – THEY'RE RUNNING AWAY!' jeered Miles.

They watched the spaceship gain height and circle the rooftops of the town. Stan's ears began to prickle.

'Actually, I don't think they are,' he said.

The spaceship was coming back, swooping down low towards them. Suddenly it opened fire, raking the car park.

'Yikes, that was close!' gasped Stan, as the alien craft screamed overhead. It banked again, preparing to circle and come in for another attack. Stan looked around. They were sitting ducks in the car park, with nowhere to run.

'If you've got an idea, now's the time,' murmured Minnie.

'OK, this is the plan, kids,' said Captain
Courageous. 'Never give in!'

'Great, but maybe something more
practical,' sighed Minnie.

Stan thought quickly. If only they could
create a magnetic force field or something.
Wait a minute, maybe they could? He felt in
his pocket for the
packet of bionic
bubblegum.
It was
their only
chance.
Tearing
off the
paper, he
jammed a
stick of gum
into his mouth,
chewing furiously.

'They're coming back!'
warned Minnie. **'DO SOMETHING!'**

'Hold on to my arms,' said Stan.

'What?'

'JUST DO IT!'

Minnie grabbed hold of his arm. Stan blew a bionic bubble, knowing it would need to be a monster to have any chance. In no time it was as big as a beach ball and growing fast.

The alien spaceship swooped down towards them, coming in for the kill.

Captain Courageous dived to the ground and shut his eyes.

The bionic bubble was so big it threatened to lift Stan off the ground. It took all Minnie and Miles's strength to hold him down.

'LOOK OUT!' yelled Minnie. **'It's going to ...'**

Moments later they opened their eyes to
see the smoking wreck of the spacecraft.

'Yikes!' said Minnie.

Miles shook his head in awe. 'That's some
bionic bubblegum!'

'It was nothing,' said Captain Courageous, who had been curled in a ball the whole time. He brushed some bits of spacecraft off his costume and smoothed back his hair.

'Who *were* those goons, anyway?' he asked.

'They were dressed like aliens.'

'They *were* aliens,' sighed Minnie. 'It looks like they were trying to steal you.'

'Well, naturally,' said Captain Courageous. 'I'm happy to sign autographs but you can take things too far.'

Miles still looked puzzled. 'But why kidnap ME?' he asked. 'I'm not even famous!'

'I guess they thought a double could be useful,' answered Stan. 'That way one of them could blend in. We knew something was up when you flew over the swimming pool.'

'I did?' said Miles.

'Well, the alien Miles did,' said Minnie. 'It must have been his job to lead them to the Captain.'

'That's why he kept hanging around in high places!' said Stan. 'He was waiting for Captain Courageous to rescue him!'

The famous superhero looked around.

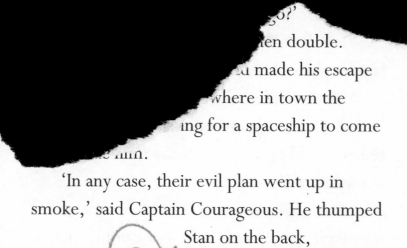

...o?'

...en double.

...u made his escape

...where in town the

...ing for a spaceship to come

...e him.

'In any case, their evil plan went up in smoke,' said Captain Courageous. He thumped Stan on the back, winding him.

OOPH!

or you

And who knows

famous as me.'

Stan sighed heavily.

he said. 'We were meant to si

today. We'll probably be thrown out

missing them.'

Miles gaped at them. 'You're not serious?
I was kidnapped by aliens – they can't fail me
for that!'

our story?

the spaceship.'

Captain

this school of yours,

Chapter

Lift Off

Miss Marbles shuffled the pile of exam papers, glanced at the hall clock and shook her head sadly.

Just at that moment the door flew open and Stan and his friends rushed in, out of breath.

Miss Marbles frowned and folded her arms. 'You're too late,' she said.

'But it's not our fault,' began Minnie.

'It's never anyone's fault, Minnie, but you know the rules,' said the head teacher. 'No one remains at Mighty High unless they pass their Heroes. I must say, I'd expected more from you three.'

'But Miss Marbles, we had to find Miles,' said Stan. 'He was captured by aliens and they were trying to kidnap Captain Courageous ...'

'And we fought them off but they attacked us in their spaceship, then Stan blew a bionic bubble and it went

EEEEEOWWW-CRASH!

and exploded – the spaceship, I mean, not the bubble,' gabbled Miles, not pausing for breath.

Miss Marbles rolled her eyes. 'And you expect me to believe that?' she asked.

'Actually, it's all true,' said a deep voice behind her. Miss Marbles spun round.

'CAPTAIN COURAGEOUS!'

she cried, clutching at her heart.

'At your service, Miss,' said the superhero, saluting her. 'I've been hearing what a terrific job you're doing at this school of yours.'

Miss Marbles blushed. 'Well, we try our best, Captain,' she said.

'If it wasn't for these brave kids, I wouldn't be here now,' said Captain Courageous. 'I might be halfway to Planet Goonie.'

Stan and the others listened while Captain Courageous told the whole story, although in his version he played the starring role, taking down the spaceship and fighting off the aliens single-handed. What mattered though was that Miss Marbles believed him. Stan thought she probably would have believed anything he said.

'Well, I must say no one's ever come up with *that* excuse before,' she said at last. 'But since Miles was in danger and you were helping one of our greatest superheroes ...' (she beamed at Captain Courageous) '... I am willing to let you off this once.'

'Thank you!' cried Minnie, hugging the head teacher round the waist. Pudding barked, reminding them his part shouldn't be forgotten.

'Nevertheless,' said Miss Marbles, 'it doesn't excuse you from passing exams like everyone else. I suggest you take a seat right now and I will hand out your test papers.'

'Sounds like fun,' grinned Captain Courageous. 'Well, best of luck, kids, and keep up the good work!'

He shook hands with them all and kissed Miss Marbles' hand. (She almost fainted on the spot.)

Then he took off into the sky, forgetting that it was wise to open a window first.

Stan, Minnie and Miles sat in the front row of desks while Miss Marbles placed exam papers in front of them. Stan scratched his ear out of habit. After all they'd been through, an exam didn't seem so daunting. But their whole future at Mighty High would depend on the next hour and the answers they gave. Miss Marbles glanced at the clock.

'You may turn over your papers and begin!' she said.

HEROES LEVEL ONE

Answer the questions by ticking one box.

1. It is a superhero's duty to …

a) Save himself

b) Save for a rainy day

c) Save the world

2. One of these three could be a criminal – but which one?

a)   b)   c)

HEROES LEVEL ONE

3. Which of the following is NOT on the list of 20 Most Wanted Supervillains?

a) The Green Meanie

b) Doctor Sinister

c) Shadowman

d) Lollipop Man

Stan finished the last question with five minutes to go and checked over his answers. To be honest, the exam hadn't been half as bad as he'd feared. In fact, many of the questions only required common sense (though that probably ruled out a few people passing, like Tank, for instance).

Miss Marbles collected their papers, adding them to the pile on her desk.

'Excellent,' she said. 'So that's the written exam over. Now all that remains is the practical.'

Stan's heart sank. He'd forgotten about the practical – and they all knew it involved flying.

In their lessons with Professor Bird, only Miles had flown, and he was an alien at the time so it didn't really count. What chance did they stand of achieving lift-off now?

Miss Marbles led them on to the stage and brought out a stopwatch.

'It's very simple. I'd like you to remain airborne for ten seconds,' she said. 'Jump, float, fly – it doesn't matter as long as you're off the ground. I shall be timing you.'

Stan looked at his friends helplessly.

This test could only end in failure. He'd never flown in his life, so he wasn't likely to start now.

'How did the others do?' asked Minnie.

Miss Marbles sighed. 'Not one hundred per cent success,' she admitted. 'But still, no bones broken.'

Miles's shoulders drooped. 'This is impossible,' he muttered.

'Think,' urged Minnie. 'It's only ten seconds; there must be a way.'

'Yes, if you're Captain Courageous,' said Miles.

'I'll give you one minute to prepare,' said Miss Marbles. 'Who wants to go first?'

Stan tried to remember Professor Bird's advice. *Let go; imagine you're light as a feather.*

But it hadn't helped when he'd fallen off the high-diving board. Nor had the bionic bubblegum – though come to think of it, that was probably their only hope. Maybe if he blew a monster bubble it would keep him airborne for ten seconds?

'Bionic bubblegum. I've got just one stick left,' he said, showing the others.

'That won't work; there's three of us,' said Miles.

'You try it, Stan,' said Minnie. 'At least one of us can pass.'

'No way, we're the Invincibles! We stick together,' said Stan. 'When I nod, grab hold of me and try to breathe in. We have to be as light as possible.'

He put the bionic bubblegum in his mouth and began to chew.

'Ready?' asked Miss Marbles.

Stan nodded and blew a blue gummy bubble. In seconds it grew so big that Miss Marbles stepped back to get out of the way.

Stan kept blowing till the bubble started to lift his feet off the ground. He waved to Miles and Minnie, who grabbed hold of him around the waist.

'It's no use!' moaned Miles.

'We're way too heavy!'

'Take off your belt and boots!' cried Minnie.

The bubble grew and grew, wobbling like a giant blue jellyfish. Stan was running out of puff. Finally they felt a tug as they lifted slowly off the ground.

'It's working!' whooped Minnie.

They floated up towards the ceiling, with Miles and Minnie hanging on to Stan's waist.

Below them, Miss Marbles counted off the seconds.

'Seven, eight, nine ... **TEN!**
That's it, TEN seconds, you've
passed!' she cried. 'You can come down
now!'

They'd reached the ceiling, where the

bionic bubble was stuck like ... well, like
bubblegum.

'Brilliant! We did it!' said Minnie. 'So
how do we get down?'

Stan hadn't thought that far ahead. He'd
got them up in the air; getting down was
another matter. 'Wait,' said Miles. 'Surely
sooner or later bubblegum is bound to ...'

HAVE YOU READ THE FIRST

SuperHero School

ADVENTURE?

See opposite for a sneak peek!

Chapter 1
Dangerboy

Dangerboy's cape whipped around him. The city spread out below like a rumpled red duvet.

Mrs Button poked her head round the door. 'How many times? No jumping on the bed!'

'But Dangerboy has to save mankind from Dr Doom!' said Stan.

'Well, tell Dangerboy his dinner's getting cold.'

Stan sighed. By now Dr Doom would be halfway to his secret volcano lair. Stan peeled off his superhero mask and hung it on the bedpost. He'd have to finish saving the world after dinner.

Halfway downstairs he stopped and scratched

his left ear. It was tingling, which probably meant sprouts for supper.

'Come on, lad, we're hungry,' said Mr Button, looking up.

'I had to practise my surprise attack move,' said Stan. 'Dr Doom was getting away . . .'

'Well, if he's a doctor, he's probably very busy,' said Mrs Button.

Stan sat down and looked at his plate. His tingling ear never failed.

Mr Button speared a chip on his fork. 'Have you given any thought to what you might like to be if you don't become an – um – superhero?'

'I'll be a superhero,' said Stan without hesitation.

'Yes, but it's good to have other options,' said Mrs Button.

'And it's good to have ambition,' Mr Button sighed. 'But not everyone can be a superhero. Do you actually know any superheroes?'

'What about Captain Courageous?' said Stan.

Every week the *Gormley Gazette* reported on Captain Courageous's latest daring adventures. Stan had pictures and posters of him all over his walls. Beside his bed was a plastic model of the superhero that he'd got free in a packet of cornflakes.

'Exactly,' said Mr Button.

'What do you mean?' asked Stan.

'Well, he can fly and he's got superpowers. It's difficult to learn things like that.'

'Maybe he started off by jumping on the bed too,' said Stan. 'Then one day he discovered he could fly. That's why I need to practise.'

'What for?'

'So that I'm ready,' said Stan, smearing a chip with ketchup. 'You don't know – I could get a call at any time.'

A letter came through the door and landed on the doormat.

Mrs Button went into the hall and returned holding a long silver envelope with no postmark or stamp, just a name and address.

'Ooh, it's for you, Stan!' she cried.

'Me?' Stan looked up. He never got

letters – except when he had an overdue library book. But this didn't look as if it came from the library; it looked exciting.

Well open it then

Stan tore the envelope open. Inside was a letter written in purple ink. It was short . . . and baffling.

MIGHTY HIGH SCHOOL

Dear Stanley Button,

It is my great pleasure to invite you to attend an interview at Mighty High School.

Please come at 9.30 am prompt. I very much look forward to meeting you.

Yours sincerely,

Miss M Marbles
(Head teacher)

P.S. I mean tomorrow!